For Matthew
—CL

For Sven
—GH

tiger tales
an imprint of ME Media, LLC
202 Old Ridgefield Road, Wilton, CT 06897
Published in the United States 2003
Originally published in Great Britain 2003
By Little Tiger Press
An imprint of Magi Publications
Text copyright ©2003 Christine Leeson
Illustrations copyright ©2003 Gaby Hansen
CIP data is available
ISBN 1-58925-027-3
Printed in Singapore
1 3 5 7 9 10 8 6 4 2

Molly and
the Storm

by Christine Leeson
Illustrated by Gaby Hansen

tiger tales

It was the first sunny day after weeks and weeks of rain.

"Can we go out to play, Mom?" asked Molly Mouse, dancing in the pale sunshine. "Please?"

"As long as you keep an eye on the weather," said Mother Mouse. "I'm sure more rain is on the way."

Molly and her brothers and sister scampered across the fields. They chased each other around trees, puffy and white with blossoms.

They hopped through carpets of bluebells.

They were enjoying themselves
so much that they didn't notice it
was suddenly getting darker.

Plop!

A large drop of rain fell on Molly's nose—then another and another. Big dark clouds filled the sky, and the rain started to fall faster and faster.

"We'll never get home in time," groaned Molly. "Where can we find shelter until it stops?"

Just then, a squirrel hurried by
on her way home. She stopped when
she saw the wet little mice. Her own
family was safe and warm in their
nest. She couldn't possibly leave the
mice out in the rain.

"Come with me," she said. "You
can stay at my place."

Squirrel ran ahead and bounded up
a tree, but the mice didn't follow.
"Your house is too high and it doesn't
look safe in this storm," sighed Molly.

An old harvest mouse popped her head out
of the long grass.
"You can stay with me," she said kindly. "I have
a nice warm nest of twigs."

Harvest Mouse scuttled to her home, but the mice didn't follow. They could see that her woven nest was far too small for all of them.

Just then a little rabbit found the mice. "You can come to my place," cried Rabbit, "and join my baby brothers and sisters in the warmth of our burrow." He couldn't leave these poor little mice out in the storm.

Rabbit hopped down his rabbit hole, but the mice stayed outside. "Your home is very full," said Molly, peering inside at all the baby rabbits. "I think we'd be too squished."

Before Rabbit had time to answer, he and the mice heard someone calling. Molly pricked up her ears.

"It's Mom!" she squeaked.

"Thank goodness I've found you!" cried Mother Mouse. "The storm is getting worse. But there's an old hollow oak tree nearby where we can stay dry until the rain stops."

The hollow oak tree stood at the top of a slope. The mice scrambled inside and were soon warm and dry.

"We'll stay here tonight," said Mother Mouse. "You can all curl up together and go to sleep."

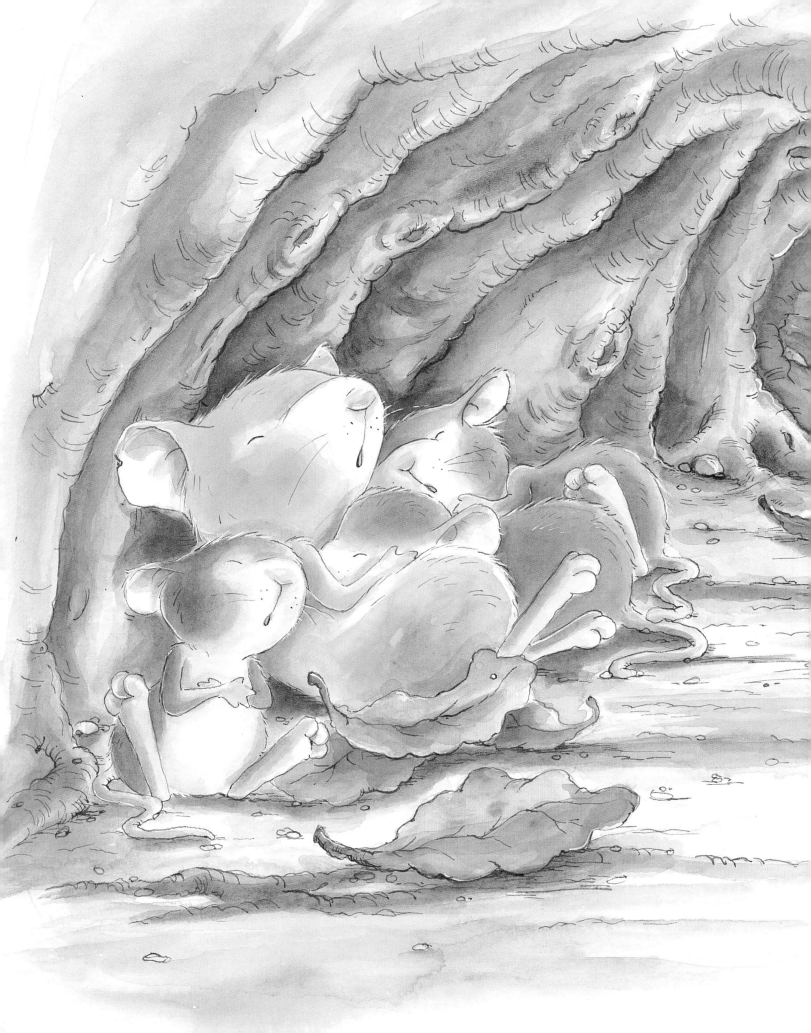

But Molly couldn't sleep. She lay listening to the roar of the wind and the pounding rain, and she was worried about her new friends. Would Harvest Mouse's home be destroyed? Rabbit's burrow might be flooded, and Squirrel's nest blown away.

Molly looked at her family, sleeping snugly. She couldn't leave her friends out in the storm. Molly hurried outside.

The wind tugged and pulled at Molly
as she struggled across the field. There,
huddled under a swaying tree,
was Squirrel.

"You must come
with me," said
Molly. "We
found the
perfect place
to stay."

Just then, Harvest Mouse appeared out of the grass, looking tired and messy.

"Can I come too?" she asked.

"Of course," said Molly.

As they made their way back, they passed Rabbit and his family huddled under a bush. "You'll be nice and warm if you come with us," said Molly.

At last Molly and her new friends reached the shelter of the old oak tree. Outside, the wind battered the trees and flattened the grass. But inside, everyone was safe and dry.

The wind had stopped by the time morning came, and as the sun crept up into the sky the animals crawled out of their shelter. There before them was a rainbow, stretching as far as the eye could see.

"It's for you, Molly," whispered Harvest Mouse. "It's a special present for saving us."

And Molly smiled happily, surrounded by her family and all her new friends.